WALTHAM FO

This book should be retu
the last date stamped be
Provided that the book is
required by another reader
be renewed by quoting the
date and the number shown
below.

1992			
16. MAR 1992			
23. APR. 1992			
28. MAY 1992			
21. AUG 1992			

King of Spuds

A WOODSIDE SCHOOL STORY

King of Spuds

JEAN URE

Illustrated by
LYNNE WILLEY

**ORCHARD
BOOKS**
London

Text copyright © Jean Ure 1989
Illustrations copyright © Lynne Willey 1989
First published in Great Britain in 1989 by
ORCHARD BOOKS
96 Leonard Street, London EC2A 4RH
Orchard Books Australia
14 Mars Road, Lane Cove NSW 2066
1 85213 089 X
Printed in Belgium

Chapter 1

"And now," said Miss Lilly, "for the last few minutes before we go home . . . hands up for a game of Hangman!"

Hands shot up all across the classroom. Alison Webb turned, ready to prod at anyone who wasn't co-operating, but there wasn't any need: everybody liked playing Hangman. People like Catherine Onslow and Bader Khan, who were good at spelling, were so eager they were almost falling off their chairs. Even the Zombies gang were in favour. Cameron Philips was smashing his hand on the table top, the other three clattering their feet and bunching their fists in the air.

"Hangman! Hangman!"

(The Zombies weren't particularly good at spelling; they just liked the idea of anything which sounded violent.)

The only person who didn't put his hand up was Nicky Edwards. He saw Alison looking at him, and Shirin Shah getting her ruler out, ready to jab. There was only one thing to be done: Nicky clutched dramatically at his throat and made a gargling noise ... aaaaargh! Kelly Flanagan, who sat next to him, immediately giggled and did the same. Shirin huffed a bit, and looked threatening, but decided against actually jabbing. Nicky Edwards was the class clown: you expected him to fool around.

"Well!" said Miss Lilly. "That looks like overwhelming support ... a hundred per cent, if I'm not mistaken!"

She obviously hadn't noticed that Nicky's hand was down.

Miss Lilly divided them up, girls against boys. (Last time it had been first-half-of-the-alphabet-against-second: with both Nicky Edwards *and* Kelly Flanagan, not to mention Robert Costello, the first half hadn't stood a chance.)

"All right," said Miss Lilly. "Catherine, choose a word for your team, then come out here and be hangman."

After a bit of whispering, Catherine wrote something on a sheet of paper and began handing it round amongst the girls. One of the Zombies tried to snatch at it as it went past.

"Darren, if you do that again," said Miss Lilly, "I shall count it as a mark against your team."

All the Zombies glowered, and Cameron yelled, "You don't get nowhere without trying!"

"True," said Miss Lilly. "But if you try

cheating and get yourself caught, then you must expect to pay the price. Ready, Catherine?"

Catherine said yes. She took a piece of chalk and on the board made seven dashes.

"So it's a word of seven letters," said Miss Lilly. "Where shall we start? Robert?"

Nicky's heart went *thunk*, down into his shoes. If they were starting with Robert

Costello that meant there was only one way to go: straight on to Nicky. If they'd started the other side of the room the blanks might have been filled in before they reached him.

"Come on, then, Robert!" Miss Lilly smiled, encouragingly. "Say a letter."

Robert said, "A." He always said A even if someone else had already said it.

"No A!" Catherine shook her head. On the board she wrote:

and drew the first line in the hangman.

"Nicky?"

Cameron Philips began thumping again on the table. "Give us a vowel! Give us a vowel!" His fellow Zombies took up the chant: "We want a vowel! We want a vowel!"

"No helping!" shrieked Alison Webb.

"Cameron, be quiet," said Miss Lilly.

Cameron turned his head, so that Miss

Lilly couldn't see. "*Vow'l.*" He mouthed it at Nicky across the room.

Nicky licked his lips. He hadn't realised that a vowel was a letter. He'd thought it was a doing word. Or was that a verb? He couldn't remember! Nouns, vowels, verbs, they all got muddled inside his head.

"We-want-a-vow'l! We-want-a-vow'l!"

A familiar sense of desperation stole over Nicky. There was only one thing to do when you were in a tight corner: fight your way out of it. That was what Uncle Ted always said. Thinking of Uncle Ted inspired him.

"Ere y'are, lady!" He pushed back his chair and scrambled on to it. "Luvly ripe vow'ls! Fresh today! Take your pick!"

Catherine and some of the other girls started laughing.

"Five for fifty!" shouted Nicky, getting carried away. "Choose your own, many as yer like!"

11

Everybody was laughing now, except a few people such as Shirin Shah, who was too superior, and Bader Khan, who was too solemn (and probably wanted to get on with the game).

"Nicky! Stop creating diversions," said Miss Lilly, though she was laughing, too. "Say a letter!"

"Z," said Nicky.

The Zombies groaned, loudly. A frown wrinkled Bader Khan's forehead. Catherine, still giggling, said, "No!" and jubilantly added another line to her hangman.

"Stupid *git!*"

"Cameron," said Miss Lilly, "please don't use that language. Bader?"

Bader leaned forward, looking very earnest behind his glasses. "E."

"No E!" sang Catherine.

Nicky couldn't help being just a little bit pleased.

By the time they had gone right round the class and come back again to where they had started, the situation on the board looked like this:

Bader was biting his nails. He knew now what the word was, but Miss Lilly had made it a rule that no one was allowed to shout out of turn. (Games had been ending too quickly, because people like Bader and Catherine had kept guessing almost at once.)

"Robert?" said Miss Lilly. "Back to you again. Say another letter."

Robert said, "A."

"We've already had A, you stupid—"

"*Cameron!*"

Cameron subsided, muttering. Darren Waters kicked at a table leg.

"Have another go," said Catherine.

"*No!*" Alison and Shirin shrieked it in unison.

Soozie Schuster said, "He's had his go."

"I'm afraid that's true," said Miss Lilly. "Nicky? It's up to you!"

Just one letter left. Bader knew what it was. Even the Zombies knew what it was.

O M _ I B U S

Nicky swallowed. There couldn't be that many letters that hadn't been tried; could there? Secretly, on his fingers, under the desk, he went through the alphabet: A, B, C, D, E, F—

Nobody had said F.

"F," said Nicky; and he cackled in a mad sort of way as he said it so that if it turned out to be wrong they would think he had done it on purpose, just to fool around.

"You idiot!" screamed Cameron.

"How could it be F?" Bader turned to him, genuinely puzzled.

"*Omfibus*?" bawled Cameron. "What's an omfibus?"

"Omfibus, omfibus—" Nicky wriggled his nose up and down, making snuffling noises. "Australian field mouse."

Catherine obligingly giggled as she added the final line to her hangman. Cameron glared.

"What you on about? Australian field mouse?"

"Goes omfibus, omfibus all through the

night . . . keeps all the other animals awake. All the koalas and that. Makes 'em livid."

"Show me in a dictionary," said Miss Lilly, "and I will believe you! Bader, do you want to tell us what the word is?"

Bader, sitting back in his chair, weakly said, "Omnibus."

After omnibus, Ben Morrison chose the word *wicket*, which the girls worked out in no time at all. The Zombies were furious with Nicky. When school was out they surrounded him, threateningly, in the playground.

"You do that again," said Cameron, "an' I'll bash yer!"

The Zombies thundered off, hooting and hallooing, crashing into people as they went. Bader Khan appeared. He looked at Nicky, uncertainly.

"Thought you'd like to be the one to guess it," said Nicky.

Bader shook his head. He seemed worried. "It was for the team," he said.

Team. Nicky slung his anorak over his shoulder, dangling it with one finger through the loop. He kicked moodily at the playground gate. He didn't reckon he was a team sort of person. Like Uncle Ted: Uncle Ted wasn't a team sort of person. Uncle T—

"Hey! Nicky!" He turned. Kelly Flanagan was scudding across the playground towards him, plaits bouncing as she ran. He stopped, and waited for her. "Nicky—" Her face had gone all pink; whether with exertion or embarrassment he wasn't sure. "Is there *really* an animal called an omfibus?"

"Course there is!" Nicky switched back, automatically, into his routine. "Australian field mouse, innit?"

"I told her!" Kelly flung her plaits back, triumphantly. "That Shirin Shah ... I *told* her!"

Chapter 2

The following week, some of the girls started agitating to play Hangman again.

"We could give 'em a return bout, miss!"

"Return *bout*?" said Miss Lilly. "Really, Alison, I think you must have been watching too much boxing!"

"No, but couldn't we, miss?"

"Show 'em we can beat 'em twice!" Jackie-Lee Gibbs turned and stuck her tongue out at Cameron.

"I'm not at all sure," said Miss Lilly, "that all this competition is a good thing."

"It is! It is!"

All the girls were jumping up and down.

Even Pavindra was joining in. Nicky looked at her, gloomily: Pavindra was usually so *quiet*. This stupid Hangman was really getting to them.

"Go on, miss! Please!"

"Well . . . I don't know," said Miss Lilly.

"Oh, go on, miss!"

"Let us!"

"*Please!*"

"Oh, all right!" Miss Lilly gave in, just like she always did. Jackie flashed a triumphant leer in Cameron's direction: Cameron put his fingers up. "We'll play it

tomorrow," said Miss Lilly, "just the one more time. But from then on we're going to play *co-operative* games. All doing things together; not against each other. Right?"

"No! Boo!"

They shouted in chorus; even Catherine and Pavindra. Who ever would have thought they could be so bloodthirsty? They were almost as bad as the Zombies.

At break the Zombies came up to Nicky. They surrounded him, in a circle.

"You just remember what I told you," said Cameron. "Any more messing around—"

Nicky made his eyes go big with pretended terror. "And what, oh, master?"

"And you're for it!" said Cameron.

Nicky covered his face with his hands. "Don't hit me, don't hit me!"

"Shuddup!" said Cameron.

The Zombies hulked off, doing their special Zombie walk, shoulders hunched, hips rolling. They thought it made them look dangerous. Nicky took his hands away from his face and put them up by his ears, waggling his fingers. He wasn't scared of the Zombies. Them and their stupid threats! What worried him far more was Bader. Bader wasn't a special friend of Nicky's— Nicky didn't really have any special friends; for all his clowning he was a bit of a loner— but Bader was someone Nicky respected. He wished there was something he could do to impress Bader.

That afternoon, when Nicky got home, he found his dad outside the flats with his ladders and buckets. Nicky's dad was a window cleaner. He had a contract with the local council to clean the windows of all the council blocks in their part of the borough. It kept him busy the whole year: as soon as

he'd finished the last block it was time to go back and start again.

"I dunno!" he cried, when he saw Nicky. "It's a life!"

Nicky's dad was always saying it was a life. He didn't reckon much to cleaning windows. Before he had become a window cleaner he had been a jockey, riding in all the big races, but that hadn't worked out. He'd kept falling off and breaking things. He'd broken his collar bone five times, and had a steel pin in his shoulder, which gave him terrible aches and pains in the winter; but for all that, he said, they'd been good days, when he'd been doing the jockeying. A sight better than cleaning windows.

"Whatever you do—" he wrung out his leather, slopping water on the ground— "never become a window cleaner! How was school today?"

"All right," said Nicky. His dad was always asking him about school.

"That's the ticket! Keep it up!"

Depressed, Nicky took the lift to the sixth floor. He wished his dad didn't have this thing about school. His mum had it, too.

His mum was there at the door as usual, waiting to greet him.

"Hello, chuck! Get yourself in. How was school? All right? Good! That'll please your dad. Poor love, he's in a right state. Shoulder's playing him up ... whatever you do, young Nicky, don't ever become a window cleaner. Get yourself an education, your dad's quite right. Wash your hands, now,

25

your tea's on the table. I'll just take a cup downstairs, cheer him up."

That night, in bed, Nicky dreamed of men cleaning windows as they dangled from nooses. Bader Khan was down below, looking worried and wearing three pairs of horn-rimmed spectacles, whilst overhead flapped two hideous black crows, perched on broomsticks. As the crows came closer Nicky could see that they were Alison Webb and Shirin Shah. The air was full of their bloodthirsty shrieking: "Hangman! Hangman! Hangman!"

Next morning, as soon as he woke up, Nicky knew something. What he knew was that he wasn't going to go in to school. It wasn't something that he lay there thinking about. It was something that he *knew*.

He said goodbye to his mum, as usual, and clattered down the stairs to the ground floor. He walked out through the Estate, also as usual; but when he came into Violet Lane (where once, about a century ago, there had been violets growing) he deliberately turned right instead of left. Left would have taken him to school: right took him down Greenbank Avenue, up Pond Street, through Dunnett's Yard and into the market. Half-way along the market was a stall which said ED. TRANTER, QUALITY VEG. Ed. Tranter was Nicky's Uncle Ted, his mum's younger brother.

Uncle Ted was everything that Nicky would like to be when he grew up: big, broad-shouldered (so broad were Uncle Ted's shoulders that sometimes he had to walk through doors sideways, it was the only way he could get through) with lots of dark curly hair, on his chest as well as on his head, a big booming voice that could make itself heard from one end of the market to the other, and a deep, rich, gravelly laugh which made his belly shake. Nicky would give anything to be like Uncle Ted.

At half-past eight in the morning the market wasn't yet properly awake; only the odd one or two stallholders were doing business. The rest were still sipping their mugs of tea from the market caff as they set

up. Madge, on Sea Foods, caught sight of Nicky and waved.

"Hi, there, stranger! Haven't seen you for a while. Come to give a hand?"

Other people turned, and also waved. Most of them knew Ted Tranter's lad— "my mascot", Uncle Ted called him. Nicky liked the market; he felt at home there. Far more at home than he did at school.

Uncle Ted had already set up and was drinking his mug of tea as he waited for customers. His face broke into a broad grin as Nicky approached.

"Well, if it's not me little mascot! I've not clapped eyes on you for a bit. Bin keeping your nose to the grindstone, have they?"

"Bin in school," said Nicky.

"Oooooh!" Uncle Ted shook his head. "Sounds painful! So what you doing here, then? Never tell me you've skived off!"

"Teachers are on strike," said Nicky.

"Are they, now? So aren't I the lucky one!" Uncle Ted gave his deep, rich, belly-shaking laugh. "I could do with a bit of a helping hand. D'you reckon they knew that? And that's why they organised to go on strike?"

"I don't think so," said Nicky, carefully.

"Just a coincidence, eh?"

"I reckon so."

"Ah well!" Uncle Ted winked at Nicky over the rim of his mug. "We'll not complain, will we?"

Nicky was never quite sure whether Uncle Ted really believed the things that Nicky told him—strikes, extra holidays, government cuts—or whether he just pretended to. He never said anything to Nicky's mum. The first time Nicky had stayed off school and spent the day down the market ("special holiday 'cos of the cuts") he had suggested to Uncle Ted that perhaps there wasn't any need to mention it to his mother. Uncle Ted had agreed that maybe there wasn't. He had said, "Mum's the word!" and he'd laughed.

Uncle Ted wasn't a nutter about education the way that Nicky's mum and dad were. Uncle Ted said that he'd got by all right without it, hadn't he? Stall in the market, his own house (with a garden), caravan, car, tumble dryer, video ... it was more than a lot of people had.

It was certainly more than Nicky's dad had. That was why Nicky's dad didn't want Nicky to be a window cleaner. But there wasn't any reason why he shouldn't have a stall in the market and be like Uncle Ted.

"It's a grand life," said Uncle Ted, "for them as can take it."

Nicky could take it! He'd already proved that he could. He would prove it again today. He squared his shoulders, trying to make them as broad as Uncle Ted's.

"So what's special? What's on offer?"

Uncle Ted said that Guernsey toms were today's specials, with avocado pears and asparagus going at knock-down prices.

"Avos 30p, sparrergrass £1 a pound ... fancy holding the fort for a bit? I just want to nip along down and see old Tolly Potter about a horse."

Nicky nodded, eagerly. When Uncle Ted went off to see Tolly Potter about horses he was sometimes away for as long as an hour. Nicky didn't mind: he liked being left in charge. He gathered some of the better looking avocados into a scoop and advanced purposefully into the centre of the street.

"Avos! Lovely ripe avos! Pick your own, 30p each, lovely ripe avos!"

Nicky stayed all day at the market. At lunch time Uncle Ted went off and Aunt Jenny came instead. Aunt Jenny said, "You'll catch it, you will, staying off school like this."

"They're on strike," said Nicky.

"Oh, yes?" said Aunt Jenny. "First I've heard of it!"

At quarter to four, just when he was thinking that he ought to be going home (before his mum could start worrying, and wondering where he was) Nicky had a fright: he saw Miss Lilly, with her shopping bag, come out of Dunnett's Yard and walk across to the egg stall. What was Miss Lilly doing here? She must have whizzed out of school the very minute classes ended! Nicky dived out of sight, behind a stack of wooden crates. He watched as Miss Lilly bought her

eggs. To his horror, she then turned and
began moving towards him. She was going
to come to the veg. stall!

No, she wasn't. She had moved on — she
was going to Mrs Grisby on flowers. Nicky
bolted. He didn't *think* Miss Lilly had seen
him, but it had been a narrow escape.

Chapter 3

Next morning at breakfast, Nicky's dad was there.

"Is it a holiday?" said Nicky. His dad was never there at breakfast; not during the summer. He liked to get out during the summer and make an early start.

His dad said, "Holiday? What's a holiday?"

"He's having a bit of time off." Nicky's mum shook cereal into Nicky's bowl and pushed it towards him. "His shoulder's playing him up ... can't lift his arm, poor love."

"Can't lift it at *all*?"

"Not far enough to clean windows."

"How far?" said Nicky.

With difficulty, and lots of grimaces, his dad lifted his arm about as high as the top of the cereal packet. Nicky's eyes widened. "What you gonna do?"

"That," said Nicky's dad, "is the ten thousand dollar question ... what am I going to do?" He looked at Nicky's mum as he spoke. Quickly she put out a hand and covered his.

"We'll manage. We always have before."

"It's never been this bad before. What if—" There was a long pause. Nicky stared from his dad to his mum and back again to his dad. "What if it means I'm finished? For good and all?"

"Then I'll have to make shift, won't I? I'm not helpless, you know!"

"I know you're not! I don't need telling! But you shouldn't have to—it shouldn't be this way!" Nicky's dad banged on the table with his left fist. The cereal packet jumped into the air and fell over. "Just you take note, my boy." His dad nodded sternly at Nicky across the breakfast table. "This is what happens when you don't get an education ... I don't want you muffing your chances like I muffed mine!"

"He won't," said Nicky's mum. "He's a good lad, our Nicky. And he's a bright lad, too! He'll make out."

"Not without an education, he won't. You know what I'd like for that boy? I'd like to see him get to university. Be a lawyer. Be a doctor. Something of standing."

Nicky shot an alarmed glance at his mother. Get to university? Be a lawyer? Be a doctor? Nicky didn't want to do anything like that! He wanted to go in the market, like Uncle Ted!

"Something with a bit of polish," said Nicky's dad. "Something I can be proud of!"

"He's doing his best," said Nicky's mum, "he can't do more. Eat up your cereal, love, it's time you were off." As she saw Nicky to the door, she gave his arm a reassuring squeeze. "Don't you fret about your dad . . . he'll be proud of you, whatever you do."

Chapter 4

"Ah, Nicky! There you are," said Miss Lilly. "And what happened to you yesterday?"

"Wasn't well, miss."

"No? What was wrong with you?"

"Upset tummy, miss."

"Oh, dear!" said Miss Lilly. "I wonder what can have brought that on?"

"Dunno, miss."

"You don't think, perhaps, that you've been eating too many tomatoes?"

Tomatoes? Why pick on tomatoes?

"Don't like tomatoes," said Nicky.

"Really? How odd! I thought everyone liked tomatoes. Especially the Guernsey

ones. Guernsey toms!" Miss Lilly chirruped it, happily. For a moment she sounded almost like Aunt Jenny. "They're the best ones, aren't they? At this time of year?"

"My mum buys them big ones." That was Claire Paddon, butting in. "Them beef ones. Enormous, they are. Big as apples."

"Yes? Well, I like the Guernseys," said Miss Lilly. She turned back to Nicky and held out a hand. "Have you got your note?"

Nicky assumed a blank expression. He was good at blank expressions. "Note, miss?"

"From your mother. Now, Nicky! I've told you about this before. If you're going to be away—"

"I forgot, miss."

"*Again?*"

"I'll remember next time, miss. Honest!"

"I'm very much hoping, Nicky, that there won't *be* a next time. Because if there is—" Miss Lilly paused. "If there is, we really shall have to do something about it. Right!" Miss Lilly clapped her hands. "Daily dozens! Let's get them over with."

Miss Lilly turned to the board and began to write.

228 + 154 − 137   Tom has 20p
26 × 10
16 + 29 + 28 + 19   Ann has 40p
300 − 100

wrote Miss Lilly.

Already people like Bader were busy writing down the answers. Nicky hadn't even started! Miss Lilly had told them lots of times that it wasn't a race, people could take just as long as they needed; but if Nicky were to take as long as he needed he would still be sitting there at going-home time.

Usually, when he saw that everybody else at his table had finished, he just started guessing and wrote down anything. That way, only Miss Lilly would know that he still hadn't learnt how to add up and take away and do multiplication. (He lived in dread of Bader discovering. He couldn't bear the thought of Bader knowing how stupid he was.)

After doing the daily dozen, they had to read their Mike and Patsy books. There were hundreds of Mike and Patsy books— well, it seemed like hundreds when you'd only managed to get through three of them and still had another great huge stack to go. Catherine Onslow and Pavindra Patel had actually got through the whole lot. Not even Bader Khan had done that.

Nicky was on *Mike and Patsy and the Great Jumble Sale Robbery*. It was supposed to be quite exciting. Sophie Waters had seen it and said, "Oh, that's a good one! That's fun." Nicky didn't find it fun. It was full of long words like cardigan, which he couldn't read. It made it very slow-going.

He managed to stagger through another three pages and then it was break. Break was OK; he didn't mind break. After break they had singing. That was also OK, even though Nicky couldn't sing, but then neither could Bader Khan: Bader Khan sounded like a car horn in agony. The Zombies, with the exception of Ben Morrison, who to everyone's surprise had turned out to be musical, sounded like a whole chorus of car horns. Soozie Schuster was tone deaf. On the whole, Nicky quite enjoyed singing.

After singing there was lunch, and after lunch, for the first half hour, they did

projects. Nicky was working on a project about wombats. He was in the middle of drawing one (trying to make it look a bit more like a wombat and a bit less like a furry tea cosy) when to his horror he heard Alison Webb say, "Can't we play it just once more, miss? Just once, to get our own back?"

She wasn't on about Hangman *again*?

"Please, miss! It's only fair!"

"Best of three, miss! They always do best of three!"

This time, to Nicky's relief, Miss Lilly stood firm. "I don't care if they do best of three hundred. I told you ... no more competitive games!"

"Oh, miss! Go on!"

"Your one idea," said Miss Lilly, "seems to be to wage war on each other!"

"YES!" The Zombies and the Spider Gang roared it in chorus.

"There you are, you see! I knew it was bad for you."

"But you got to try and beat other people," said Alison, "haven't you?"

"Why?" Miss Lilly looked at her. "What do you want to beat them for? Just stop being so aggressive all the time! I have a new idea for this afternoon."

"Something with teams, miss?" That was Kelly Flanagan, who didn't always listen; or if she did, didn't always understand.

"No, Kelly, this is not with teams!"

"Spelling?" said Catherine, hopeful.

"Not spelling, either . . . I think we've had enough of spelling for the time being. This is going to be something quite different."

"Boys against girls?"

"Nobody against anybody!"

"Not even alphabetical?"

"No, Kelly, not even that."

Nicky relaxed, and went back to his wombat. So long as it wasn't teams, or spelling—

"So what is it, miss? This game? If it's not spelling . . . what is it?"

"Well, now!" Miss Lilly closed the register and pushed back her chair. "I suppose you would say—" She thought for a few seconds. "I suppose you would say that it was mathematical!"

Chapter 5

Mathematical? Nicky stared, in horror. He wasn't the only one: several people had their eyes popping out and looks of disgust on their faces. Even Catherine Onslow's jaw had dropped. Bader Khan, on the other hand, had taken off his glasses and was energetically polishing them on the end of his tie, getting himself ready. Bader liked maths. So did Alison and Shirin. They were smiling, smugly.

"Can we start it now, miss?"

"Yes, all right," said Miss Lilly. "Why not?" She seemed really turned on by the idea. Really excited. "Put your projects away; you can go back to those tomorrow. Now! Everybody up! You girls, I want you to take all the chairs and stack them in the corner; we don't need chairs. And I want the boys to move the desks so that they're in two rows, facing each other, across the middle of the room ... that's it, Cameron! That's right! Leave a bit of a gap between them— enough for people to walk through. And quite a lot of space between the two rows. I want it to look like a street."

Like a street? What was mathematical about a street?

"Come on, Nicky! Do something! Now, let's see ... how many tables are there? Six. Right! Let's have Soozie—" Miss Lilly crooked a finger at Soozie Schuster— "Sandra, Alison, Ben, Bader, and ... Nicky!"

Nicky felt his stomach begin to churn. What was this? Something else horrible that

he wouldn't be able to do?

"Out you come!" cried Miss Lilly. "I want each of you to stand behind a table: those are your stalls." Nicky blinked. "*Stalls,*" said Miss Lilly. "As in a market! Right? I shall give you each a piece of card, and on that card I want you to write your name and what you're selling, so that everybody can see. Nicky, what are you going to sell?"

Nicky tried to find his voice, but it

seemed to have disappeared somewhere down the back of his throat.

"How about vegetables?" said Miss Lilly. Nicky nodded, dumbly. He was feeling rather confused. "All right, then! Nicky's going to sell vegetables. Soozie, how about you?"

Soozie Schuster said she was going to sell jewellery, Alison said fruit, Sandra Martin said, "Eggs."

"Just eggs?" said Miss Lilly.

"Different size eggs."

"I hope they're all free-range," said Catherine. "I shan't buy any if they're not."

Sandra said yes, they were all free-range. Ben said so were his live eels that he was going to sell. The Zombies sniggered. Catherine immediately turned pink and looked as if she might be going to cry. Catherine hated anything that was cruel to animals, even wriggly things like eels. Miss

Lilly said, "I don't think we want a live eel stall, Ben. You can have whelks and cockles, if you like. Bader?"

Bader said he was going to sell books, so that was all right. While the rest of the class decided what sort of shoppers they were going to be—"You don't necessarily have to be yourselves," said Miss Lilly. "You can be anyone you want"—the stallholders settled down to write their cards.

N. Edwards
Fresh Veg

wrote Nicky, in the curly sort of writing that Uncle Ted used for his stall. Miss Lilly then went round handing everyone little piles of pretend money, which she must have borrowed from the class below them. (They had spent a lot of time playing with pretend money when they were in the class below.)

"All you stallholders can count up what

you start with, then count again at the end and see how much you've made. But remember," said Miss Lilly, "this isn't a competition! Now, then ... I declare this market open. Off you go!"

There was a moment's silence, while everyone stood around looking at everyone else, waiting for somebody to do something. Some of the girls giggled. Then Nicky, bundling a handful of imaginary avocados into an imaginary scoop, marched forth boldly into the middle of the desk-lined street.

"Avos!" bawled Nicky. "Lovely ripe avos! Take your pick!"

Jackie-Lee Gibbs came up, dragging Diane Evans by the hand and slapping her as she did so: Jackie was being the mother and Diane was her child.

"Stop that row, I've told you before! Take that!" WALLOP, went Jackie: SCREECH,

went Diane. "All right, my man, I want half a pound t'maters, three pound taters, two pound carrot, an' a good firm cauli."

"Half a pound t'maters, three pound taters, two pound carrot, good firm cauli, one pound twenny."

Jackie looked at Nicky, suspiciously. "How d'you make that out?"

"T'maters 50p a pound, taters 5p a pound, carrots 20p a pound, that's 80p, plus 40p for your cauli. Next, please!"

Catherine giggled: she was too shy to play at being anyone else. All she wanted was a pound of peas. Nicky gave her the peas— "They mightn't be much to look at, but you'll find they shell beautiful!"—and turned to Shirin Shah. Shirin Shah wanted to know if he had any aubergines. (Shirin Shah *would*.) Nicky said no, they were too expensive, not worth buying; whereupon Shirin sniffed and flounced off to the fruit stall to ask for passion fruit.

Kelly Flanagan then came and wanted "eighteen pounds of the best potatoes", which was ridiculous because she couldn't possibly have carried them, but she insisted so he gave them to her. Some people just had no *idea*.

Cameron Philips tried to cheat him: he handed over a five pound note and then complained that Nicky had given him the wrong change.

"I don't think Nicky's likely to do that," said Miss Lilly. "He's good at this sort of thing, aren't you, Nicky?"

Was he? Nicky's cheeks, beneath their freckles, grew slowly scarlet.

"That's *favouritism*!" shouted Cameron; but nobody took any notice except for Ben Morrison, who threw an imaginary shellfish at him.

"Well, now!" said Miss Lilly. "I think it's time I bought something ... how about a bunch of that lovely asparagus that you sell?"

"Sparrergrass?" Nicky perked up. "Got plenty o' that!"

"So how much is it?"

Nicky thought about it. "£1.50."

"A bunch?"

"Fresh today, you won't find better!"

"You did say £1.*50*?"

"That's what I said, lady!" Nicky was

61

beginning to enjoy himself. "Take it or leave it!"

Catherine gasped. Soozie Schuster giggled. Nicky, growing daring, said, "At £1.50 I'm giving it away!"

"Yesterday," said Miss Lilly, "you were giving it away for only a pound."

There was a pause. Nicky looked at Miss Lilly; Miss Lilly looked at Nicky.

"Goes up and down," muttered Nicky.

"So what do you think it's likely to be next time?"

Nicky swallowed, and shuffled his feet. It was a wise man, according to Uncle Ted, who knew when he was beaten. "Won't be any next time, miss."

"No?"

Nicky shook his head.

"Are you quite sure about that?" said Miss Lilly.

"Yes, miss."

The other stallholders seemed puzzled. Sure about *what*?

Miss Lilly knew.

"In that case," said Miss Lilly, "we have cause for celebration." She took out her purse. "Give me a bunch of your extremely expensive asparagus!"

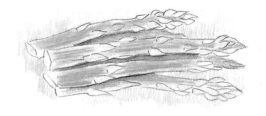